The Magic Island

Written by Julia Zheng

Illustrated by T. K. Diem Nguyen

The Magic Island

First printing edition, 2021

Library of Congress Control Number: 2021917306

ISBN: 978-1-7375146-7-1 (pbk)

Printed in the United States of America

This book is dedicated to my nephew Leon (Chinese name 郑乐炎), who is my inspiration for the main character, and to all the children who love to dream.

Contents

Chapter 1
To the Magic Island

"Leon, I'm going to the farmer's market. Remember to finish your homework," Leon's mother said as she left the house.

"Okay, Mom. I will," said Leon, sitting at a desk by the window.

Leon Lee was a seven-year-old Hawaiian boy of Chinese origin. He lived in Hilo, Hawaii, with his mother, Sabrina Lee. Leon had his mother's bright brown eyes and soft, dark hair. He loved to use his imagination to draw pictures and show them to his two best friends, Malo and Crystal. They enjoyed looking at Leon's drawings.

Summer vacation was Leon's favorite time of the year because he was free to spend his days with Malo and Crystal, who lived right next door. The three of them liked playing sports, going to the beach, riding on their bikes, or playing hide-and-seek in the yard.

The two months of summer had flown by. Leon sat by the window on his last day of vacation, thinking about the school assignment he still had to do—write about something memorable that happened during his vacation. He racked his brain, but couldn't think of anything interesting enough to write about.

Suddenly, outside the window, he saw a giant bird chasing a flying creature. It zipped about, but the bird was faster and eventually caught it in its beak. Determined to save the prey, Leon rushed outside. He picked up a rock and threw it at the bird. Scared, the bird dropped the creature, and it landed on the grass in the yard.

Leon went to see if it was okay.

There, on the grass, sat a cat-like creature wearing a messenger hat with a feather tucked into the side. Its body was snow-white with eyes that were striking and unusual—one green, one blue. Leon wondered whether this little creature was a cat or not. Its ears were big, and its tail was round and short.

"Are you okay?" Leon asked as he carefully helped the chubby little thing up.

"I suppose so," said the little creature, standing up and shaking his head.

"You can talk. Wow!" Leon was amazed.

"Of course I can. I can speak many languages. Thank you for saving my life, by the way." The little creature bowed to Leon sincerely.

"Don't mention it. I saw you flying with a white machine. What's that?" Leon asked curiously.

The little creature pointed at the feather in his hat and said, "This is my flying feather."

"That's amazing. You can talk and fly. Are you a fairy or a genie?" asked Leon, his eyes wide open in wonder.

The little creature slapped the dust and grass off his body and said, "My dear fellow, allow me to introduce myself. I'm a messenger from the Magic Island. My name is Alto. As an enchanted cat, I'm different from the ordinary cats you know."

"Nice to meet you, Alto. My name is Leon. Are you bringing a message to someone?"

"Oh, right. I think so. But I don't remember to whom I'm bringing a message." Alto rubbed his sore head. "I must have hit my head harder than I thought."

"Do you at least remember the message?"

"Let me think... I think I was going to invite some guests to our island, or I believe that was the message."

"How far is this Magic Island? Can I come?" Leon asked excitedly.

"It's quite far," Alto warned. "But since I forgot my guest list, and you just saved me, I'd love to bring you instead—if you want to."

"Cool!" Leon exclaimed. "What about my friends, Malo and Crystal? Can they come too?"

"Are they nice kids like you?"

"Yes, they're nice like me, and they live close by."

"Should we go and invite them?" Alto asked politely.

"Yes, please."

"Okay, but I think my back is a little dirty from the grass," said Alto. "I'd like to look proper in front of your friends. Your shirt looks nice, Leon."

"Thank you. This is my Peter Pan outfit. My mom made it for me because she knows how much I love Peter Pan."

"How sweet of her! I think I've got an idea," said Alto as he took off his hat and blew on it. Suddenly, the hat turned green. Then he blew on his body as well, and a green shirt like Leon's appeared.

"Wow!" said Leon in awe.

Alto smiled at Leon, then rubbed his paws together and said, "Off we go."

They went to Malo's house first and found him playing soccer in the yard by himself. Malo Woods was a native Hawaiian boy with chin-length brown hair and eyes the color of the deep ocean. He loved to surf and play sports.

"Hey, Leon, come play with me," Malo said, kicking the ball toward Leon.

Alto caught the ball with both of his feet, having flipped his body upside down.

"Malo, come here. I have news for you."

Malo ran toward them, "What's up, Leon? When did you get a cat, and how can he catch a soccer ball like that?"

"No, this is not my cat. This is Alto. He's a messenger from the Magic Island. He invited us to go there!"

"Nice to meet you, Malo," said Alto as he flipped his body upright again.

"Nice to meet you too, Alto. Wow, a talking cat! And a magic island? That sounds fun. Let's go ask Crystal too. She must be so bored practicing the piano," said Malo.

The three of them arrived at Crystal's house. Through the window, they saw her playing the piano by herself. Crystal Waters had long, blonde, curly hair that rippled down to her waist like a waterfall. Today she was wearing a white doll dress with a sunflower bow in her hair.

Leon knocked on the window. Crystal smiled when she saw her friends and came to talk to them at the window. "Leon and Malo, what are you doing here?" Her big green eyes shone in the sunlight as she spoke.

"Crystal, come with us. We're going to the Magic Island. It will be more fun than playing the piano at home."

"I'd love to, but I don't think my mom would allow it," said Crystal.

"Not to worry," said Alto, "I have this." Alto took off his hat and pulled a clock from it.

"What's that, Alto?" Leon asked.

"This is a Time Frozen Clock. Once I press the button on the top, time will stop anywhere within ten miles of this clock. When you come back, it'll still be the same time as when you left. You just need to press the button again to restart time," Alto said as he pressed the top button of the Time Frozen Clock. It instantly vanished.

"Is this real? Leon, this cat is talking and doing magic!"

"Yes, Crystal. This cat is my new friend, Alto. He is going to take us to his island."

"Sounds great! I love cats," said Crystal. She went to grab her favorite doll before joining the others outside.

"How do we get to your island, Alto? Is it somewhere far away?" asked Crystal.

"Yes, it's far away, so we'll fly there," said Alto.

"But how?" the three children asked together.

"With this," said Alto. The next thing they knew, Alto threw his feather up high. It grew bigger and bigger and bigger until Alto said, "Stop."

"Wow!" exclaimed Crystal. "It's big enough to ride!"

"But feathers don't fly," Malo reasoned. "Birds do."

"This one does," Alto assured them. He took a magic controller out of his hat and lowered his flying feather to the ground.

"All right, everybody on board."

Leon, Malo, and Crystal were all so excited. They jumped inside the feather cabin right away. Alto placed the little controller in the front of the flying feather and blew on it. The controller turned into a steering wheel.

In no time, the flying feather was up high in the sky, and the three little friends cheered. They didn't know what kind of surprise was waiting ahead, but the view up in the sky was cool enough to blow their minds.

Alto, now the captain, seemed to be quite experienced at driving the flying feather. "Hold on!" he said. "We're going to sail on the water." Gradually, the flying feather landed on the water and started to sail like a boat.

Not too far away, they saw a bright light.

"We're almost there," said Alto.

From a distance, the Magic Island looked like a land inside a bubble dome. The whole island sparkled.

Moments later, they landed by the side of the island. The flying feather became smaller and smaller. Alto and the three children were about to fall into the water when a giant octopus caught them with her arms.

"Let me go! Let me go!" Crystal screamed.

Alto quickly said, "Don't worry, kids. This is our friend and the gate guardian, Cleo. She makes sure that everybody lands safely."

The giant octopus carried them above the water's surface to the island and let them down. Meanwhile, the flying feather had changed back to the size of a regular feather, and it flew back to Alto's hat by itself.

"Thank you, my dear Cleo," said Alto to the giant octopus.

"Anytime. Welcome to the Magic Island, little fellows!" Cleo said to the three children.

"So, this is it?" asked Leon.

"Yes, welcome to the Magic Island!" Alto exclaimed. "Please allow me to show you around our wonderful kingdom."

Leon, Malo, and Crystal all clapped. They couldn't wait to start their tour of this dreamlike place.

Chapter 2
The Spring Garden

Following a path lined with colorful flowers, the four of them reached a gate that was the shape of a rainbow, and each stripe of the rainbow had flowers in the same color lined up together.

Alto explained, "This is our first stop, the Spring Garden. Our whole island is divided into four sections, and each section has its own people and creatures. We all live happily and free, except for the war we once had."

"There was a war? What happened?" asked Leon.

"It's in the past. No need to bring it up again. Now everything is peaceful and safe," Alto assured them.

The three children felt relieved.

Alto opened the gate. In front of them was a sea of giant flowers, cotton candy trees, vibrant green grasses, and tasty-looking fruits. It was so colorful and beautiful.

"Wow!" Crystal couldn't help but run into the field. The rest followed. There were giant flowers everywhere, with leaves as tall as houses providing shade. Leon and Malo climbed up to the top of the flower petals and bounced on them. They offered to help Crystal climb up, but she was more interested in a field with steps in the same shape of piano keys. As soon as her foot touched the grass, she heard a piano note similar to: "do." When she took another step, she heard a higher piano note: "re."

"This grass can play music!" Crystal told Leon and Malo.

"Yes, this is the Piano Field, Miss Crystal. You can use

your feet to create any music you like," Alto said with a smile.

"This is so much more fun than playing my piano at home!" said Crystal, stepping all over the piano field.

Leon and Malo joined in. Soon, the garden was filled with musical notes, though without much rhythm.

The flower buds heard the music and blossomed into smiling faces.

A line of giant golden bees started to collect nectar.

A flock of swallows came to form a chorus.

Butterfly fairies emerged and danced with their glittering wings fluttering about them.

"Those bees are so much bigger than the ones in our yard," said Malo.

"And their wings sparkle," added Leon.

"Would you like to take a ride on the golden bees?" asked Alto.

"Can we?" responded the three of them excitedly.

"Sure," said Alto. He whistled to the bees, and four of them flew over to him.

"Hey, Alto. What's up?"

"Hi, Bee H. My friend would like to take a ride. Would you guys be so kind?"

"Certainly! Hop on." Alto introduced the bees as Bee H, Bee I, Bee J, and Bee K. They landed on the grass one after another in a straight line. Malo was so excited. He climbed up as quickly as he could. Leon helped Crystal climb up onto the bee's back first, then climbed up himself.

Off they went. The bees, Alto, and the children flew under giant flowers and over giant leaves. The view in the Spring Garden was incredibly pleasant, with all the green grasses waving and the flowers blooming. The

birds, chipmunks, and squirrels who all lived together in the treehouses came out to greet them.

Suddenly Crystal's stomach rumbled. "I'm getting a little hungry," she told Alto. "Is there anything to eat?"

"Of course, my dear. Bee H, please take us to the Fruit Field."

"All right, hold on tight." Bee H and the other three bees made a left turn, and soon they arrived in the Fruit Field.

Leon and Malo jumped down by themselves. Alto helped Crystal climb down slowly. Then he went to take a nap in a hammock made of spider webs.

"Children, help yourselves. All the fruits are organic."

The three of them ran to pick the fruits they liked. There were all kinds to choose from on the ground or up in the trees.

"Come and look at these grapes!" Crystal called to Leon and Malo.

She showed them a bunch of grapes containing the seven colors just like the colors of the rainbow—red, orange, yellow, green, blue, indigo, and violet.

"Are those grapes edible?" Leon turned to ask Alto.

"Of course, children. They're delicious."

Crystal was so hungry that she ate a whole bunch of grapes.

"They're sweet and sour. I love them!" she told Leon and Malo happily.

The boys had some too. Then, they went off to look for their own fruits. Leon found some heart-shaped apples, while Malo climbed the candy bar trunk of a short cotton candy tree.

"Hey, Crystal, do you want some of this cotton candy?"

Malo reached up to pick some of the cotton candy from the tree, and he saw the part he picked immediately grow back.

"That's awesome!" he said.

Leon saw a yellow frog jump out of a pond. He crouched down to talk to the frog. "Hey, Mr. Frog, why are you yellow?"

"I'm yellow because I live in this pond. This is the Pond of Color. When you touch the water, your skin will become a different color depending on which patch of color you touch."

While the yellow frog was speaking, a pink frog jumped out of the pond.

"Malo, Crystal! Come here!" Leon shouted. "Would you like to try this?" he asked, pointing to the water's surface. "This pond can change our skins' color, just as it did for those frogs."

"I'm not so sure," said Crystal. "What if I can never change back?"

"You have nothing to worry about, Crystal. You will still be you even if you change the color of your skin. I will try first. But can you tell us if there's a way to change back to our normal skin colors, Mr. Frog? If yes, how?" asked Leon.

"That's easy," said the yellow frog. "Right in the middle, lies a patch of clear water. When you touch that, your skin will return to your normal color."

"That sounds fun! I want to try," said Leon, dipping his hand into the green patch of the pond. Slowly, his skin turned greener than the leaves around them.

"That's so cool!" Malo said. He put his hands into the blue patch of the pond, and his skin turned blue.

"Come on, Crystal. Don't you want to try it too?" asked Leon.

"Okay, but I want to see your skin color change back to normal first," said Crystal.

"All right, we'll show you."

Leon and Malo wanted to touch the clear water in the middle of the pond, but they couldn't reach it. The pink and yellow frog came to help. They jumped into the clear water, and the water splashed Leon and Malo. Instantly, they returned to their normal skin colors.

"Now you can try, Crystal," said Leon.

"All right." Crystal touched the pink patch in the pond, and she turned pink. She laughed at her new look. Then she touched the violet patch. This time, she became violet.

After that, Crystal changed back to her normal skin color, with the help of the frogs.

The three children wanted to play a trick on Alto. So, they scooped up a little water from the yellow patch of the pond with a leaf and splashed it on Alto's body while he was still asleep. Alto's body turned yellow.

The children's laughter woke Alto up. He looked at the new color of his fur and said with a smile, "You naughty children!" He walked to the Pond of Color, made his feather bigger, and used it to scoop some clear water up. As soon as his hand touched the clear water, his body turned back to white.

"Alto, we've had so much fun in the Spring Garden. You said there are four sections on this island. When are we going to the second section?"

"We can go now if you want."

The children nodded eagerly.

"Follow me!" Alto said, leading the children to their second destination.

Chapter 3
The Summer Palace

They arrived at a gate with seashells shaped to form the words *Summer Palace* on both sides.

"Children, here we are," said Alto after they stepped inside. "This is the Summer Palace. The temperature is always hot here. The Sand Boys, whose bodies are made of sand, live here. They love to play with coconut balls on the beach."

"Were the Sand Boys made in the same way snowmen are?" asked Leon curiously.

"They weren't made by humans, my dear. When our goddess, Numa, first came here, she felt lonely as she had such a beautiful view but nobody to share it with. So, she used the sand to make many little people and brought them to life with her power."

"Will they melt like snowmen?" asked Crystal.

"They will melt if they meet water, but it never rains here."

"Then how do the plants stay alive?" asked Malo.

"Look over there. We have a waterfall that runs forever." Alto pointed to a waterfall behind them, and then he whistled. Suddenly, five blue elephants appeared and used their trunks to spread water on the plants.

Scuttling out from the bushes, a crab came from behind and lifted Alto up in the air.

"It's me, Mr. Crab! Let me down, please?" Alto said.

"Oh, it's you, Alto. Why are you wearing a shirt today?" asked Mr. Crab, putting Alto down.

"I got the idea from my new friends here."

"I see. That's cool, Mr. Messenger. Who are these little fellows?"

"These are my friends, Leon, Malo, and Crystal."

"Welcome to the Magic Island!" Mr. Crab clapped with his two big claws.

The children all smiled. They couldn't wait to tour the Summer Palace.

"Come on, children," Alto said. "Let me show you how wonderful this place is."

As they walked on a beach of colorful sand surrounded by tropical plants, they saw giant watermelon houses everywhere—each had one door and two windows.

"What are those for?" asked Malo.

"Those are the houses for the Sand Boys. They dug the flesh out from the giant watermelons and made the watermelon rinds their houses. A long time ago, Goddess Numa had used her power to make those watermelon houses solid and dry like a rock."

"Can we meet the Sand Boys?" asked Leon.

Alto nodded. "Sure, but they're very shy. They usually hide themselves on the tops of the palm trees," said Alto.

"We're friendly, though. You can tell the Sand Boys that," added Crystal.

"Don't worry. The Sand Boys like to play. They will come out by themselves," assured Alto.

As they continued their walk, a coconut suddenly dropped to the ground, almost hitting Malo's head.

"That was close," said Malo. The four of them looked up, only to find a Sand Boy making a face at them.

"Do you think the Sand Boy tried to hit us?"

"No, no, no. They're just playing. They meant no harm," said Alto. "Come down, Sand Boys. Come and meet your new friends."

A dozen Sand Boys, as flexible as monkeys, climbed down from the palm trees.

Alto and the three children were soon surrounded by many Sand Boys, who were less than two feet tall and had seashell eyes, noses, and mouths. Each of them wore a pair of red rain boots and a skirt that was made of palm tree leaves.

"Would you like to play coconut ball with us?" asked the leader of the Sand Boys. He wore a crown made of leaves.

"Sure, I'd love to," Malo said first.

"I'll join too," said Leon. "How about you, Crystal?"

"Actually, I'd love to watch you play." Crystal felt a little tired from the heat.

Leon and Malo joined the Sand Boys to play coconut ball. They were divided into two teams. Each team needed to get the coconut ball from the other team and kick it into the holes in the ground that the crabs had dug. Alto was the referee.

After a while of watching the boys play coconut ball, Crystal grew bored. She walked to a rock by the water and settled there near the gentle waves. As she enjoyed the cool breeze off the ocean, she saw a little mermaid waving to her.

"Hello, I'm Miya. What's your name?"

"I'm Crystal. Nice to meet you."

"Nice to meet you too. Your hair is so long and beautiful, like a golden waterfall. Can I braid it?"

"Sure, if you want to."

Miya braided Crystal's hair into a single braid. Crystal looked at her reflection in the water and said, "It looks so cute this way. I love it! Thank you, Miya. You're so sweet. I'd love for you to have my doll as something to remember me by."

Miya accepted the gift with a smile. She and Crystal cheered for Leon, Malo, and the Sand Boys as they watched them play.

Soon, night came. They all slept inside a watermelon house after having a delicious dinner of fruits, including yellow strawberries, green peaches, and iced coconut milk mixed with hot cocoa.

The next day, they said goodbye to the happy Sand Boys and continued to their next destination.

Chapter 4
The Autumn Forest

Four flamingoes gave Alto and the three children a ride on their backs. In no time, they arrived at a gate built in the shape of a giant maple leaf.

"Here we are," said Alto, jumping down from the flamingo's back.

"Autumn Forest," Leon read out loud.

"Yes, this is the Autumn Forest. You'll find more food here as this is the place of harvest."

"Who lives here, Alto?" asked Leon.

"The hard-working Woody People. The Woody People have many machines that make different kinds of food."

"Let's go see them!" said Malo.

The four of them entered through the gate and walked into the Autumn Forest. There were red and yellow trees everywhere. Surprisingly, no leaves were found on the ground except the prints of maple leaves on each brick. The children looked around in wonder.

"Why do my feet feel warm, Alto?" asked Crystal.

"The Woody People installed heat systems under the ground. They are very smart. They can adjust the temperature to the degree they want for different creatures. When they saw us coming, they turned the temperature up," explained Alto.

"How nice of them!" said Crystal.

Before long, they saw a fountain with *Milky Fountain* written on it. Leon took a sip and said, "It really is milk in this fountain!"

Malo and Crystal drank some too.

Alto said he did not like milk, which the children thought was odd for a cat.

After the children finished drinking the milk, they saw a field of mini trees with bread buns growing on their branches.

The three children ran to pick some to eat, as they were all so hungry after only eating fruits.

"I've never seen bread grow on a tree before," said Crystal.

"Alto, there is a lot of bread here. Can the Woody People eat it all?" asked Leon.

"No, they don't eat the bread themselves. The Woody People send most of the food they grow to other islands in the feather boats for the poor people," explained Alto.

"What else do they grow?" asked Malo.

"The Woody People grow and make food in different ways. Come, let me show you more!"

They arrived in a cornfield and met the guide, a three-eyed turkey.

Alto said to the children, "Go pick some corn and try it."

After trying one, Leon said, "This corn kernel tastes like candy."

"Mine tastes like honey," said Malo.

"Mine tastes like chocolate," said Crystal.

Alto smiled. "Yes, this is the sugar corn the Woody People planted."

"Can we meet them?" asked Leon.

"Sure, they live in the pumpkin houses on the other side of the cornfield. But before we reach the pumpkin houses, we have to cross the River of Time."

"What's the River of Time?" asked Malo.

"I'll tell you when we arrive."

"Okay," said the children together.

On their way to the river, the children met monkeys playing on the swings and deer skipping rope. Everyone seemed very happy.

Soon they reached a narrow river with a single-plank bridge across the middle.

"Do we have to cross this tiny bridge?" asked Crystal. "I can't swim."

"You always have us, Crystal. We'll save you if you ever fall into the water," Leon said with a smile.

Crystal was happy to hear that.

"Don't worry. This river is very shallow. You can cross it if you want to, but this isn't a regular river. The reason it's called the River of Time is because it can show you the past and the future if you step into it," explained Alto.

"Really? How?" asked Leon.

"If you step into the east side of the river, you can see what will happen in your future on the surface of the water. If you step into the west side of the river, you can see what happened in your past on the surface of the water. You just need to think about what in your future or past you want to know. The answer will appear on the water. Children, do you have anything you want to know about the past or the future?"

"I want to know what I'll become in the future," said Malo.

"I want to know what happened to my father," Leon said. "My mother never really told me the details. She just said he died in an accident."

"It's up to you, but the River of Time only gives you one chance to see your past or future. If you wish not to know anything, you can just cross the bridge."

"I don't want to know anything," claimed Crystal.

"Why not?" asked Alto.

"I like surprises, and my past is great the way it was," said Crystal.

Crystal and Alto crossed the bridge first.

Malo stepped into the east side of the river. The water was only up to his knees. On the surface of the water, he saw that he would become a surfer in the future, just as he had expected. Then he stepped up to the bank where Alto and Crystal were.

"I must practice harder so that my surfing can be excellent," said Malo.

Leon took a deep breath and stepped into the west side of the river. On the surface of the water, he saw that his father had lost his life while fighting some bad people on the street.

Leon wept after he saw what had happened. Alto, Malo, and Crystal comforted him.

Alto said, "There is always evil in this world. You just have to be strong and fight for what's right."

Leon wiped away his tears and nodded in agreement.

Together they kept walking until they reached the giant pumpkin houses with spider web windows.

They knocked on the door of one, and a Woody Person opened the door.

The three children couldn't tell if this Woody Person was a boy or a girl, as it had a body made of wood and springs and a face like a robot. It had two horns instead of hair, and both its legs and arms were rather short.

"Oh, it's Alto, my friend. Please come in."

"Hi, MuMu. These are my new friends, Leon, Malo, and Crystal. They're visiting our island as guests."

"Welcome," said MuMu, whose horn became long enough to shake the children's hands.

The three children looked around the pumpkin house and saw chairs made from cotton flowers and a bed that looked like a giant silk cocoon.

"May I ask if you are a boy or a girl, MuMu?" asked Leon.

"I'm neither. We Woody People don't have a gender."

"Then how do you make a baby?" asked Crystal.

"Come with me, I'll show you," offered MuMu, walking out of the pumpkin house to the backyard.

There, the children saw lots of Woody People working on watering and fertilizing more food that contained juice inside instead of flesh, such as oranges and grapefruits, and fruit kabobs that grew on vine leaves.

In the middle of the yard was a pyramid-shaped lab made of transparent glass.

The camera at the front door screened MuMu's face, and the door opened after a beeping sound.

They came to a rectangular machine. "This is how we make new Woody People. I lie inside this machine, and it makes a copy of me."

"Will it be your twin?" asked Leon.

"Good question. The body can be copied, but we have to program the brain and personality with that computer right there," MuMu said, pointing to a round computer in the corner of the room.

"How long do you live?" asked Malo.

"Our bodies are made of a certain type of wood and metal, so they will only last about forty years at most. But we can program our brains and personalities to save them inside the computer. All we need to do when our

bodies wear out is make new ones and program our brains and personalities into them."

"Do you ever grow old?" asked Crystal.

"No. Woody People are always the same."

"I wish I could bring my grandpa and grandma here. They'd love to have a new body," said Crystal.

"This doesn't work for the flesh, my dear. It only applies to materials," answered MuMu.

"I see," said the children together.

After they left the lab, the children wanted to go to the last destination, but Alto said, "It's going to be freezing cold there. We should prepare before we go."

"But we didn't bring any coats with us," said Leon.

"Not a problem," replied Alto. "Let's go ask for help."

They walked to a pond where a few swans were taking a nap.

"My dear friends, may we borrow one of your feathers? We're going to the Winter Castle."

The swans all woke up and smiled at Alto. The leader swan answered, "Alto, you're our lifesaver. We'd be more than happy to help." She plucked one feather from underneath her plumage with her beak and passed it to Alto.

"Thank you, my dear," said Alto. He and the three children came back to the lab where he gave the feather to MuMu, and MuMu put it inside the copy machine and programmed the shape of coats inside the computer. Within a few minutes, four coats with wings on their backs were made for Alto, Leon, Malo, and Crystal. Each one fit perfectly.

They flew to their last destination, using the wings on the backs of their down coats.

On the way there, Leon asked Alto, "Why did the swans say you were their lifesaver?"

"One time, when I went on a trip, I saw those swans were in a factory being plucked alive to make down coats for humans. I couldn't stand the torture they went through, so I rescued them and brought them to the Autumn Forest. They've been living here happily ever since."

"That's very kind of you!" said Crystal.

The boys nodded in agreement.

They all turned their faces into the wind as they soared over the gorgeous landscape on their way to the Winter Castle.

Chapter 5
The Winter Castle

Finally, they landed in the last section of the Magic Island. As they walked further and further, they felt the wind getting colder and colder.

When they arrived at the gate of the Winter Castle, they saw it was made of two giant sparkling snowflakes.

"This is the Winter Castle, my dear friends. It's ruled by Queen Icy with her Ice Girls. Only the ones who can stand the cold live here."

"Sounds interesting. I'd love to see it, as winter in Hawaii is never too cold," said Leon.

"Me too," said Crystal and Malo at the same time.

They stepped inside the gate. Everything was made of ice. Their faces felt cold, but thanks to the down coats, their bodies were warm. There were no plants in sight, just a world made of ice.

As they explored, they saw penguins waving at them and polar bears eating something that looked like popcorn. They asked Alto what it was.

Alto told them it was Snowflake Popcorn. It tasted like popcorn mixed with ice cream. The Ice Girls made them with their magic hands.

As they walked closer to an ice castle, they saw many girls made of ice with hair like icicles. They had transparent bodies and huge eyes. Their feet were shaped like blades, skating on the icy ground.

"CoCo!" Alto called to one of the Ice Girls.

"Hey, Alto. Long time no see," replied the Ice Girl.

"Yes, my dear. Would you take my new friends for a ride, please?"

"Sure." CoCo whistled, and three purple unicorns showed up with a sleigh.

The children were very surprised to see the unicorns. They came closer but were a little nervous about patting them. These three unicorns looked a little different from the ones they'd seen in books. Their bodies were made of ice and their horns were made of hailstones with glittering red light. They did not make any sound but were smiling at the children.

"Come," said Alto.

The children were so excited as they climbed onto the sleigh. The ride was nice with lots of giant fireflies flying around and the bright glow from the three unicorns' horns lighting up the path, as this place was dark with no sunshine.

During the ride, Leon asked, "Alto, were those unicorns made by Goddess Numa too? I often wondered if they actually existed."

"Yes, they were made by Goddess Numa. The original unicorns live in the Rainbow Castle in the Heaven Kingdom. When Goddess Numa created the Magic Island, she thought the light of the unicorns' horns would've been helpful in the Winter Castle. Since she wasn't allowed to move them here, she used her magic power to create many of them out of ice. They now live in the Purple Castle."

"How I wish I could have a pet unicorn!" said Crystal.

"They don't like to be kept as pets. They enjoy their freedom. And that's another reason Goddess Numa made Magic Island their home: they're free here. Our queen is

like a mother to all of us. Everyone is equal here on our Island."

"We're glad to hear that!" said Malo. "Can these unicorns talk?"

"No, they don't use language. They prefer silence. They only use body language to communicate, especially their horns."

"How do they use their horns to communicate? Do you mean the lights?"

"Yes, Leon, you're very close. They can feel each other's feelings through their horns. The horns change color depending on the unicorn's mood. When they're happy, it's a red light. When they're sad, it's blue. And when they're scared, it's gray."

The children nodded, amazed.

"We're about to reach the Purple Castle," Alto reminded the children.

The children couldn't wait to see more unicorns.

After a right turn, a purple ice castle came into view. There were a few unicorns resting outside. Their horns were red in the beginning but turned white when they saw the children.

"What do the white horns mean, Alto?" asked Crystal.

"Miss Crystal, it means they don't recognize you."

"But how come these three unicorns' horns were always red, even when they first saw us?" asked Malo.

"Because CoCo transferred the message that you're our guests through her whistle. So they weren't startled."

Once Alto waved to the unicorns, their horns turned red again. The children were amazed at the way some of the creatures communicated here.

On their way, they passed a hot spring with a giant white turtle inside.

"What is the turtle doing in the hot spring?" asked Leon.

"He is healing himself from the illness. This is the Healing Hot Spring. Just like humans, animals here get sick sometimes. So, Goddess Numa created this Healing Hot Spring for them. Once they sit inside the Healing Hot Spring, their ill bodies start to heal."

"Mr. Turtle, how are you doing?" Alto asked.

"Oh, hello, Alto. I'm doing better, thanks to the Healing Hot Spring."

"Glad to hear." Alto smiled at Mr. Turtle and so did the children.

"I see you've got some new friends here," Mr. Turtle said slowly.

The children all waved at Mr. Turtle.

"Yes, they're our guests and have been wonderful friends too."

"That's nice. Maybe I can show you guys around when I feel better?"

"That would be lovely. Thank you so much, Mr. Turtle," said Leon.

They continued their ride and soon passed the ice castle they'd seen earlier.

"Would you like to see Queen Icy?" Alto asked.

The children nodded.

Alto made the unicorns stop the sleigh. The unicorns nodded goodbye with red horns and went back to their Purple Castle.

Alto and the children stepped inside the lobby of the ice castle. The entire place was empty except for a bed, with cold air blowing in the middle. On the bed lay a beautiful woman with an ice body and long icicles for hair. A delicate white crown sat atop her head. Her eyes were closed, and her lips were red like roses.

"This is Queen Icy," said Alto.

The children looked at the statue in front of them. Queen Icy appeared slightly fearful.

"Why is Queen Icy a statue? What happened to her?" asked Crystal.

"She was attacked and cursed by an evil monster," said Alto.

"Where is the monster now?" asked Malo.

"The monster is locked in the island prison."

"Why hasn't somebody saved Queen Icy?" asked Leon.

"Nobody could. If we ask for help from this monster, he may escape and take over the whole island. If that happens, we will all be doomed!"

The children felt awful for the queen, trapped under the curse. But what could they do?

Chapter 6
Fighting Monster Volcano

The four of them returned to the Spring Garden through the back door of the ice castle.

While Alto took a nap, Leon, Malo, and Crystal decided to go look for the prison.

Not long into their journey, they saw a rock shaped like a pair of lips and wondered at its curious form.

"I'm the Honest Talking Rock. What questions do you wish to have answered? Remember, though, you can only ask me questions now if you seek the truth. If you come back, all you'll hear will be lies." The giant rock closed its lips.

"Where is the prison on the island?" asked Leon.

"The prison is called the Well of Eternity, and it's underneath the Tree of Wisdom in the Spring Garden."

"How do we find the Tree of Wisdom?" asked Crystal.

"It's the biggest tree in the Spring Garden. Keep walking in the direction of the sun, and you won't miss it."

"If it's a well, hasn't the monster already drowned?" asked Malo.

"It's a dry well," answered the Honest Talking Rock.

"How do we see the Well of Eternity if it's underneath a tree?" asked Leon.

"The key is on the top of the tree. It's shaped like a heart. Once you get the key, you place it into the lock in the tree trunk, and you'll see the well."

The three children thanked the Honest Talking Rock and headed in the direction of the sun, looking for the biggest tree in the Spring Garden. It wasn't long before they saw a giant tree shaped like an umbrella, with a heart-shaped lock in the trunk.

"This must be it. I know how to climb a tree. I'll go get the key." Malo carefully climbed up the big tree and grabbed the key.

Leon placed the key inside the lock. The tree trunk opened like a gate, splitting halfway on each side. The children looked down and saw a well locked by a transparent, round, diamond cover. The well was so dark that the children could barely see anything.

"Anybody there?" asked Leon. He thought the monster couldn't hear him because of the diamond cover. But what he didn't know was that the monster's ears could hear through any surface, and his voice could pierce through any surface.

"Who are you?" a deep, evil voice shouted back.

"We are guests on the island. We have come to ask if you can free Queen Icy," said Leon.

"I will, if you free me first!"

"We can't. Alto told us that you will destroy the island if you are let go," said Malo.

"You must do something for me in return if you want me to free Queen Icy."

"What would you like us to do?" asked Crystal.

"First of all, give me some food. I've been hungry for years."

The children picked lots of fruits before coming back to the well.

"We have some fruits for you," said Leon.

"Good. Open the diamond door a little so you can give me the fruits."

"But what if you escape?" Leon said with wariness in his tone.

"I can't escape if you push the cover just a crack to the side so that you can give me the fruits. I'm too big to escape through a crack."

The three children believed him. They forcefully pushed the glass door to one side to drop the fruits through the tiny crack.

Suddenly, a curl of black smoke seeped through the crack.

The black smoke turned into a monster that was made of lava rocks with two eyes and all his veins burning like fire. He was about seven feet tall, and his head was flat, with the middle caved in like an upside-down cone.

"Ha-ha-ha-ha! I'm Monster Volcano, the most powerful being of all. Now, I'm taking my kingdom back! Ha- ha-ha," laughed the monster flying in the air.

The children immediately ran away screaming. Monster Volcano caught Crystal and said, "Bring me the Sword of Power in exchange for this little girl." Then he flew away, creating a flurry of wind.

Everywhere he went, the land lost its color.

Crystal was so scared that she fainted.

Leon and Malo were extremely worried about Crystal. They found Alto and asked for his help.

Alto was in complete shock. He blamed himself for not taking good care of the children. "It's my fault! If I didn't take my nap, none of this would have happened."

"It's not your fault," Leon comforted him. "We shouldn't have done anything without checking with you first. We were just eager to find a way to save Queen Icy."

Still looking guilty, Alto asked anxiously, "Please tell me how you found Monster Volcano and how he escaped?"

Leon explained everything in great detail.

"We were too naive and believed him. Now we must save Crystal!" said Leon.

"We will try, but Monster Volcano is very powerful."

"Can you tell us what happened between Monster Volcano and Queen Icy?" asked Malo.

Alto recalled, "A long, long time ago, this was an island with no creatures. Goddess Numa, who was my master and the youngest daughter of God of Heaven, was curious about life on earth, so she sneaked down by herself. The island she landed on was in the middle of nowhere. Feeling sad for the isolated land, she created the Magic Island, dividing it into four sections with different seasons. Goddess Numa created different kinds of people and creatures and then invited other creatures from outside the island, too. Everyone lived happily together. Then Goddess Numa decided to create four children to rule the island. We had Queen Bee in the Spring Garden, King Sand in the Summer Palace, King Woody in the Autumn Forest, and Queen Icy in the Winter Castle.

When God of Heaven found out Goddess Numa was absent, he ordered her to come back. And to punish her for misbehaving, God of Heaven forbade Goddess Numa to ever go back to the Magic Island. But Goddess Numa was always concerned about the island and everyone on it, so she secretly sent me down as her messenger. I can send messages to her on my flying feather, but I'm not allowed into Heaven."

"During the time Goddess Numa was on the Island, King Sand always felt that she favored the other siblings,

as he was the most fragile one. He didn't have power like Queen Bee's shooting stinger, or King Woody's wooden axe, or Queen Icy's frozen charm, and he'd melt if he met water. He became very jealous, so he went to the Island of Evil and stole the cursed lava stone after Goddess Numa left. It was said that anyone who replaced their heart with the cursed stone would become super powerful. That was what King Sand did! He put the cursed lava stone into his chest, turning himself into the very powerful and evil Monster Volcano. He returned to the Magic Island to take control of it. First, he killed Queen Bee and King Woody by burning them to death. However, when he fought Queen Icy, he discovered that he couldn't win. His fire wasn't able to melt her ice body because Queen Icy could shoot water right out of her eyes. In the end, Queen Icy caught Monster Volcano and imprisoned him in the Well of Eternity. Unfortunately, before the diamond cover was fully closed, Monster Volcano cast a curse at Queen Icy through his eyes. Queen Icy has been asleep ever since."

The children nodded in understanding.

"So, this is the war you mentioned when we first arrived here? Why didn't Queen Icy kill Monster Volcano instead of imprisoning him?" asked Leon.

"Yes, Leon, that's the war. Queen Icy couldn't kill Monster Volcano as there was only one weapon powerful enough to do so."

"Is it the Sword of Power?" said Leon.

"How did you know?" asked Alto.

"Monster Volcano told us to bring the sword to him in exchange for Crystal before he flew away," answered Malo.

"Yes, it's the Sword of Power. But nobody knows where it's hidden. God of Heaven hid it somewhere on this island in case we had enemies to defeat one day. He wanted to make sure Goddess Numa could return to Heaven without worrying about the island's future."

"Even if we find the Sword of Power, how can we find Monster Volcano and Crystal?" asked Leon.

"Don't worry. As soon as we find the Sword of Power, he'll come for it by himself."

Leon, Malo, and Alto began looking everywhere for the Sword of Power.

The giant golden bees flew all around the Spring Garden to help.

The Sand Boys searched every corner of their land in the Summer Palace.

The Woody People looked down every path in the Autumn Forest.

And the Ice Girls slid to every corner of the Winter Castle.

But the Sword of Power was nowhere to be found.

It was heartbreaking to see the whole island lose its color.

Finally, Leon, Malo, and Alto came back to the Well of Eternity.

"Maybe Tree of Wisdom will know," suggested Leon.

"Dear Tree of Wisdom, do you know where the Sword of Power is?" asked Alto.

"I don't know about that, but I can tell you what I know." A face appeared on the tree trunk.

"Please do!" begged Leon.

"The Sword of Power will only show up where love occurs."

"We love Crystal. She's our best friend!" said Leon and Malo.

"That's all I can tell you," the Tree of Wisdom said, his face disappearing slowly.

Leon's heart squeezed. He couldn't bear the thought that they might never see Crystal again, and he started to weep. His tears fell to the ground and soaked into the soil. Suddenly a bright light erupted from the ground. It was so intense that Leon, Malo, and Alto couldn't open their eyes.

A green sword grew out of the ground in front of them like a sprout.

Alto gasped. "This must be the Sword of Power!"

Suddenly, a heavy wind blew Malo to one side. Leon held on to the Sword of Power, so he didn't get blown away. Alto held on to the Tree of Wisdom, so he wasn't blown away either.

Monster Volcano appeared with Crystal.

"Give me the sword!" demanded Monster Volcano.

"You let go of Crystal first!" shouted Leon.

Monster Volcano threw Crystal to the ground and flew toward the sword.

Leon and Alto ran to check on Crystal. She slowly opened her eyes and was happy to see her friends. The three of them were relieved to find that Malo caught himself by grabbing a tree limb.

No matter how hard Monster Volcano tried to pull the sword from the ground, it did not move a bit!

"Get the sword for me, boy, or I'll kill you all!" screamed Monster Volcano to Leon. His voice was so loud that the whole island shook.

Leon didn't want any of his friends in danger, so he approached the sword and put his hand on the hilt. He lifted it out of the ground easily. The sword glittered with a shining light.

Monster Volcano flew back, trying to grab the sword. But as soon as he looked directly at the sword in Leon's hand, his eyes began to blur. He roared. Leon cowered in fear. The memory of his father's murder came back to him.

"You have to stab the sword into his heart, Leon!" Alto shouted.

Leon hesitated, his hands shaking.

"Leon, Monster Volcano will destroy all of us! Remember, fight for what's right!" Alto shouted again.

Monster Volcano made another attempt and tried to grab the sword.

An image of Leon's mother rose before him. *We must make it home safely for our families!* Leon thought. As Monster Volcano flew down for the blade, Leon summoned up all his courage and swung the sword right into Monster Volcano's chest. The sword was so powerful that the area around them turned back to its colorful form. Leon used both hands to push the sword deeper into Monster Volcano's chest.

With a strong, exploding light, Monster Volcano turned into black ashes. The only thing left was a heart-shaped piece of lava stone.

With a wave of light and color, the whole island shifted back to its original vivid form.

"You did it! You killed Monster Volcano!" Alto said to Leon.

Malo and Crystal both rushed to embrace him.

"Are you alright?" Leon asked Crystal and Malo. They nodded.

"That's unbelievable! I never thought I was brave enough to do something like that."

"You are brave, Leon. Never think any less of yourself!"

"What's this on the ground, Alto?" asked Crystal.

"This is the curse stone that put Queen Icy to sleep. Leon, break it with the sword, and Queen Icy should wake up."

Leon lifted up the sword and cut the lava stone into pieces. Once the stone crumbled to dust, the sword vanished in a glittering burst of brilliant light.

Alto and the three children went to the Winter Castle to check on Queen Icy. The queen woke up finally, and she was very happy to have been saved from her curse.

Alto told Queen Icy what had happened, and she thanked the three children. She told them they could stay on the Magic Island as long as they wanted and were always welcome to come back anytime.

"I think it's time to go home," said Leon. "We love it here, but we miss our homes more."

"Of course," said Queen Icy. "Alto will show you how to go back home. We are forever thankful that you saved our island!"

"You are welcome, dear queen. We are glad to help." Leon smiled at the queen.

Alto flew the three children back home on his flying feather after they said goodbye to everyone on the Magic Island.

"Remember to press the top button of the Time Frozen Clock to restart time," Alto reminded Leon.

"Sure, I will."

"By the way, Leon, I hit my head on the tree when Monster Volcano appeared. Now I remember what my mission was when I went to Hilo. I received a message from Goddess Numa in Heaven. She wanted me to ask help from Goddess Pele to see if she could save Queen Icy. But I think you've done a wonderful job finishing her task."

"You should thank the bird that chased you. Otherwise, we wouldn't have been invited."

"Ha-ha, you are right!" Alto hugged each of the children before flying away on his giant feather.

The three children were now back at their homes. Leon saw the vanished Time Frozen Clock was now on his table and pressed the top button. It vanished again.

It occurred to Leon that his mother wasn't back yet, as time had been stopped by the clock. Now he was very hungry, so he quickly ate a bowl of poi.

For once, he couldn't wait to finish his homework. He sat down at his desk and wrote the title: *The Magic Island...*

About the Author

Julia Zheng is a children's author from Fujian, China. She now lives in Massachusetts. Zheng graduated from Nanchang University, where she majored in English and studied Western culture. She taught English in a primary school in southern China before moving to the United States. Her teaching experience and passion  for writing have inspired her to write children's books, especially stories that convey important messages through humor, warmth, and a happy or unexpected ending.

For more books by Julia Zheng, please visit her Amazon Author Page:

https://www.amazon.com/author/juliazheng

Made in the USA
Las Vegas, NV
10 June 2023

73237646R00036